The Crab Island Murders

Alfonso was raised in a place much like this. He had a good mind for solving puzzles. He had just finished Police Academy, specialist in maritime law enforcement.

There were no open cases to be assigned. He was patrol, but had the option of investigating any cold case if he could find evidence that could lead to conviction.

He knew the area intimately in his two weeks on the job. He would get bored if he didn't find something to concentrate his talents on.

Then he found a file about four unsolved murders. On Crab Island.

It would be something to do.

Then things started getting weird. What had he stumbled onto? There was nothing on Crab Island but mangroves!

Contents

About the author

CD Moulton has traveled extensively over much of the world both in the music business, where he was a rock guitarist, songwriter and arranger and in an import/export business. He has been everything from a bar owner to auto salvage (junkyard) manager, longshoreman to high steel worker, orchid grower to landscaper, tropical fish farmer to commercial fisherman. He started writing books in 1983 and has published more than 350 books as of January 1, 2023. His most popular books to date are about research with orchids, though much of his science fiction and fantasy work has proven popular. He wrote the CD Grimes, PI series, and the Det. Nick Storie series, Clint Faraday series, and many other works.

He now resides in Gualaca, Chiriqui, Panamá, where he writes books, plays music with friends, does research with orchids and medicinal plants. He has lately become involved in fighting for the rights of the indigenous people, who are among his closest friends, and in fighting the extreme corruption in the courts and police in Panamá.

He offers the free e-book, *Fading Paradise*, that explains what he has been through because of the corruption.

CD is the discoverer of the Chadam Protocol for curing cancer.

Facebook page Ambrosia peruviana for cancer.

<u>*Rookie Maritime Cop*</u>

Alfonso Mercedes, or Alf, looked over the water at the island. Crab Island was fairly large for what it was, a mangrove head. It covered about six hectares. There were some large boulders and a lot of rocks and gravel and mangroves. There was nothing there. He had just completed a slow and careful look at the entire shoreline. It was called Crab Island, English, instead of Isla Cangrejos because a gringo named it that.

The new blue and white (the worst colors for boats. Upright, it was hard to see from above because it would blend with the clear Caribbean water. Upside down, it was the color of the sandy bottom.

Some politician thought the colors were good for police boats. They were always visible from the side.

So the outlaws or whatever could see them coming from a long way off?

Alf didn't think much of politicians.

Why he was here investigating a cold case came about when ...

"Alfonso Mercedes, you swear to uphold the law

to the best of your ability at all times and to protect the people who give you the authority to hold this position, blah, blah, blah."

A politician sure as hell wrote that oath! 'Protect the people who gave you the authority?' Not to protect all the people? Bullshit! I considered it was the people, period, who gave the asses the authority to formulate that oath!

"You are assigned to the Agua Verde area. There is a small office on Isla Frambueza and a new patrol craft that will be yours to use so long as you hold the office of investigator.

"You will be the only officer in that area. Eighty seven square kilometers. It is an area of little crime.

"This will be your duty area for a period of no less than one year. It is part of your training. You will have to cope with whatever comes up. There will be little, in all probability, but there will be some needs of a police officer. You are as close as the radio if you require aid. A helicopter can be there from the capital in less than half an hour. A squad boat in an hour twenty minutes.

"We seldom give a new officer an assignment of this responsibility, and never alone. Budget restrictions make it necessary. You have shown great ability at the academy. If we didn't believe you could handle this assignment it wouldn't be your assignment.

"If there are any questions of import here?"

"No. Thank you for your confidence in me. I won't let you down. I swear to do my job to the best of my ability, always keeping the protection of the innocent in the forefront of my mind."

They shook hands. Alf was relieved. Rico spouted the oath and didn't wait for an answer, so he wasn't required to give one.

They walked off the little stage. Enrico Gomez, the officer who stated the oath and gave the speech, put an arm over Alf's shoulder. "I saw you caught what I did with that phony oath. I like the way you gave an oath that wasn't that one.

"Now I'll tell you a little about the assignment. You can ask about anything else later.

"The Agua Verde area is mostly fishermen. It isn't a good stop area for drug traffickers, in one way. That many small islands make navigation difficult. On the other hand, that many small islands give a lot of hiding places.

"Not much happens there. You will be expected to keep unpermitted fishermen out.

"I'll tell you from personal knowledge that you will be wise to turn your eyes away from locals who fish without permits. You and I will feel the same about that. It is their home. Most of their ancestors were fishermen there, most from before the white man came to this part of the world. My grandfather was an Indigenous man. If anyone comes from outside the area, you'll make a lot of friends if you're hard as all hell on them. Charge them with the least infraction. There are so many laws on the books that you can find something illegal if they even go in there in a motorized boat. If it's not motorized, there are six pages of safety laws that we don't even read, but you can find ways to make outsiders know they would rather stay outside.

"That's a group of thirty one islands. Only four have populations of more than ten people. Nineteen have no population at all. They're mangrove heads. Isla Frambueza is the only one with more than a collection of a few houses. It has a general store and small clinic. Part of your job is on those islands. You might have to lock a drunk up in the shed one night a month or something. There may be a fight, other than the natural competition among the Indigenous men. It's not seriously a fight. It's a competition with rules and limits. It's a macho thing. They can get violent if it's over a woman – and the women can get violent if it's over a lover or husband or whatever.

"Get to know the local people. They're un-educated, but intelligent and good people.

"You file a report once a month to say nothing happened. If something happens, you file a report you clip to the monthly.

"Cover it enough?"

"There aren't any cases open out there now?"

"No. There's a file cabinet with a few cold cases, but they're mostly years old and dead. If you're thinking you'll be bored, you're right. You can investigate an old cold case or two if you like. Evidence in new cases disappears in hours there. In years? Good luck!"

"My gasolene and so forth are enough that I can stay on the water a lot? I like that."

"Unlimited. Your job is patrol. The boat is the only way to patrol. There's a fifty gallon drum of gasolene and a backup. One's always full. The general store has that responsibility. They sell gasolene to the natives. It's subsidized. There's no way those people could have a fishing business with having to pay the prices today. A conch would have to cost ten dollars to break even!"

"One other thing. There are raspberries on Isla Frambueza?" (Frambueza is Spanish for raspberry)

"Uh-huh. A native variety. Tasty, but watch the thorns."

The little office was clean and orderly. There was a radio and satellite phone (which meant satellite TV and computer access). The boat was new and trim and fast. He had two A-K47's, which made him wonder if maybe they hadn't told him quite all about the job.

Teresa Santos, the girl who would be his secretary – assuming he ever needed one – was a pretty twenty five year old girl who spoke English, Spanish and the native dialect. He was immediately interested. She saw the way he was looking at her and said, "Married, damn it! You. I like being married."

He grinned. "Damn it!"

"I have two sisters. Do you like fat or thin? One of each. The men here like bigger women, most of them."

"Shapely. Not fat."

"Ilena. I'll introduce you. You take it from there yourselves."

She showed him around the office, then around the town. He was introduced to fourteen people. He would remember their names and things about them. He'd trained himself for that.

He met Teresa's sister, Tina, which name simply didn't fit a woman who was almost six feet and two hundred pounds or more, to Alf. The sisters were part Indigena, and even Tina was more than pretty. The satin skin and long black shiny hair were beautiful.

When they got back to the office there was a beautiful fiery, very shapely girl sitting at the desk, watching a soap opera on the TV. Teresa introduced her sister, Ilena.

Alf was definitely interested. Ilena seemed to like him. He thought of possibilities.

Teresa grinned and winked. "Ilena, Alf's a horny solo, so be careful! He'll seduce you in a minute!

"Alf, Ilena's a horny sola, so be careful! She'll seduce you in half a minute!"

They joked a bit. They all had good senses of humor. Alf liked everyone he'd met.

Teresa warned him that he hadn't met a lot of people. She would try to let him know which ones were problems.

He went to his little cabin that came with the job. It was small, but comfortable. He liked the kitchen, particularly. He fancied himself a good cook.

The cabin was surrounded with numerous kinds of fruits. He knew most of them. He would always have the refrigerator full of different kinds of chichas (fruit drinks). There was a generator that served Isla Frambueza.

He settled in. He was comfortable.

He went around the town. He had a couple of

beers in a local cantina and met more people.

In the morning he took the boat out and spent the entire day looking over his area of responsibility. He met some of the fishermen from the other islands. They were cautious about him. They didn't yet know if he was a friend or a cop. A few could be both.

On one island, he saw illegal traps. They were used in the past to catch several kinds of smaller fishes. The two men on the little island didn't see that he was police until he was very close. It was too late to try to hide the traps.

Those kinds of traps didn't do any damage to the fish populations. They just happened to be included in a broad law.

He went to the dock. The men came to introduce themselves as Carlos and Rojelio Amoras. They said they hadn't seen him around before.

He introduced himself and said he was the new cop. He would be cruising the area a lot.

"It's a good thing those traps aren't in the water. I can't charge you with anything if they're on land," he said, with a grin. "Care to know a little trick?"

Carlos returned the grin. "What?"

"Those traps are illegal because there's only one way out, the way the fish came in. If there was another way out, you could each use five legally.

There are ten there, so it wouldn't change anything.

"Now, I'm not telling you anything. I happen to talk when I think. I'm thinking that a little trap tube on each would make them legal. I couldn't see if there was a hook that didn't let the trap open while they're in the water, could I?

"I'm glad they would never do a thing like that!"

Jelio looked interested. Carlos wanted to ask something, but couldn't think how. Alf saw that.

"I mean, like this little piece of bent wire that holds the gas line to the side ... what if something like that were to drop into the net just by the tube? It would hold the tube closed! Why, a person who was pulling the tap out of the water might accidentally hit it with his thumb and the tube would open and no one would ever know it had been closed!"

Carlos offered his hand. "I think we can be friends. You understand what we have to live with when the government stupidos come."

"That, I do. I was raised in Aguas Briliantes, which is a lot like here."

Jelio offered his hand.

"Well, I'm getting to know the area. I better get on with it. Have a good day." He backed out and went into the bay. He had two people there who would consider him to be a friend.

The rest of the day went much the same. He went to each little island with people to introduce himself. He didn't ask anyone if they had permits for him to check.

The next day was spent in getting to know the three other islands with people. He made sure everyone knew who he was and it was plain he was going to bend over backward to help the local people.

He had a streak of luck at Isla Piedras. A big boat with four smaller boats hooked trailer-style came to the docks for fuel. The people at the station said the tanker hadn't come and they didn't have any fuel. Next Tuesday.

He knew the tanker had been there two days ago. They had plenty.

He asked a local man about the boat.

"They came once before. We don't want them here. They use those big nets and there aren't any fish for weeks."

He went to the boat. There was a man from Jamaica who was captain. His crew were from Jamaica.

"You have permits to fish in these waters?"

"We don't fish here. We just come for fuel." That wasn't what he was told by the locals.

"I mean, do you have permits to be inside five kilometers of the coast. I know you don't have permits to take fish."

"We just came for fuel! We don't need permits for that!"

"Yes, you do. You aren't a tourist ship. You are a commercial operation that is not legal inside the limit. You are not allowed to come inside the limits.

"I'll let it pass, but don't come into these waters again. You can legally go to Capital City for fuel. Not to small islands."

The captain didn't reply. He went back inside and started backing away from the dock.

"They'll go out by the reef and start fishing. They did before. They don't need fuel. They carry more than they can use," a woman said. "You can make a few dollars. Charge them a hundred for fishing in our water."

"I'll do better than that," he promised. "They *won't* be back here again."

He went to his boat to contact main. He explained that some Jamaican fishermen were in the waters illegally. He wanted them out. Period.

"Rico Gomez is captain of that area. One moment."

Rico came on. Alf explained the problem.

"The second you see them drop a net or dispatch one of the smaller boats, call me. We'll put a stop to that!"

He waited and watched with his binoculars from just inside a small island. The small boats were all moving away from the main boat. He called Rico.

By the time they had the nets deployed a helicopter came overhead and announced they were in waters where they were prohibited. They would abandon their equipment and the smaller craft and would be outside the national waters within half an hour or would face imprisonment.

They started getting an argument. Rico was listening to all of it. He was in contact with Alf on the police line. Rico said to keep them arguing for eleven more minutes. They managed to do that. Suddenly two police boats were coming around the island from opposite directions. Another chopper came overhead. The police boats took the two men in each smaller boat aboard and put them in the cells on their craft. The big boat started for open water. The new chopper laid a line of fifty caliber shots across the bow. He stopped.

The police craft came to take the entire crew aboard. They had their own man who would take the big boat and all the smaller craft and equipment to Capital City.

"Done!" Rico announced. "Ninety days for the small boat crews and expulsion. The captain, who thinks he's a big shot, tried to bribe Lt. Quinten, so he gets a year before deportation. All equipment is now the property of this country.

"Your people need a big boat?"

"No. They could use one or two of the trailers."

"Okay. Good job, Officer Mercedes. It is noted for your record.

"Off the record, stick it to these bastards, but good, Alf!"

"Ten four. See you on the flip-flop."

"You don't make sense."

Then two weeks with absolutely nothing to do. He was now a solid part of this community.

He finally went to the file cabinet of cold cases. He would go stir crazy if he didn't find something to do, even if it wasn't likely to produce anything.

He wouldn't fool with any of it except one case that seemed to have a pattern. It was about four murders. Pretty messy. All on Crab Island.

So Alf went to Crab Island to look around.

Digging in the Past

Alf went slowly around another time. There were only three places he could see where it would be reasonably possible to get through the outer fringe of mangroves. Once past that, a person who knew how could move into the interior of the island. It would be far from easy, but there was a technique to moving in mangroves.

He went to the first. One of the bodies had been found just a few meters into the island. It was the first body noted. The man had been tortured to some extent, then chopped up with a machete. He had cigarette burns on parts of his body, as well as some telling bruises. The torture was not long-lasting, but it was there.

His name was suspected of being Arnold Smothers, a tourist/part-time resident of Capital City. He fit the description and the passport information and prints of Gerald Fethers. That was traced to Smothers. He was hiding there from the IRS in the states. He had some explaining to do about why two and a half million dollars hadn't had any tax paid on it. The money was in the bank here. He had managed to get it in and legal. How wasn't quite known, but is was laundered, no matter what.

That didn't break any laws here, and this country kept the US banking laws at arm's length. Let them get a foot in the door and they'd soon be running things. That wouldn't be so bad if they could manage their own economy. Theirs was, to put it truthfully, in the Dumpster and emerging very much too slowly.

That was two years ago. It was noted in the file that he had a mistress, Viviene Platos, in Capital City. She had not seen him since nine days before. He had gone to meet some people at a night club to discuss business. He never came back home. That had happened before. She was just now becoming concerned. It was only for two or three days before.

There was another note that said it was suspected also that he was involved in some kind of scam to steal treasures or land from the Indigenos. The persons he was seen with were known to be running such scams.

Okay. He got what he was asking for. This country didn't try too hard to catch crooks who killed other crooks. If he was killed by a victim of his schemes, that was also not investigated very deeply.

They did try to make certain that was what a case was about. There didn't seem to be much evidence one way or another on this one. "Suspected" meant exactly that. If they had proof it wouldn't be a cold case. It would be a closed case. He knew the rules when he got in the game. One such rule with these kinds of things is that you are playing for keeps.

Alf went through the testimony on affidavit. Everyone questioned was blind and stupid. To be expected from that crowd. Mistress was supposed to marry him soon. Everything went to her in a will. She demanded action by the police for a couple months, then everything died down. There couldn't be action when there was no evidence except that he was murdered. Who or why wasn't possible to determine with all the investigation was able to uncover.

There wasn't much else except monthly reports of no progress. Officer Elias kept the record up to date carefully.

That was easy! "No progress" once a month!

The next case was a Donald Granger, also a gringo. His passport and such were all in order. He had retired, bringing more than a million and a half to deposit in CD's that he lived off of. The interest was about ten times what it cost him to live. He went out in his boat and didn't come back. The boat was found on Isla Norte, where it had drifted into the tiny cove. He may have been in a minor scam or two, but it was a game kind of thing. No one was hurt who couldn't afford it.

He had been looking for land to sell to people from the states. He was sort of an unofficial agent for two suspected crooked investment companies. He was married to Vanesa Partridge just three weeks before he died. She couldn't tell the police anything. Her husband had insisted she stay out of the business. This was another where Officer Elias kept very concise records. There simply was nothing to use as a starting point. No one unusual was seen in the area. No one on the islands knew him.

That was a year and a half ago.

The next was three months later. Harold Kenneys. Slightly shady, another millionaire, same nothing. He was married to Violet Pensión, but they were estranged and would have probably gotten a divorce soon if he had lived. She said he was too tied up with the business to even notice her. She had dated a man right under his nose, simply to get a reaction out of him, but he chose not to notice. He was disinterested in sex and she was frustrated.

Officer Sergio Elias had kept fairly good records of that one. He seemed to ... *wait a damned minute! Three women with the initials V. P. were left millions by three different murder victims? DUH!*

He had his starting point. He would bet Elias had been very careful with the conditions and investigations, but little details like that would be a mile over his head. Alf knew several of that type from the academy. They were good records keepers, but useless as investigators. The records were on computer, so a correlation program would have brought the initials out – if he had known enough about the system to use it.

Alf expected the fourth, just a year and a month ago, was going to have a V. P. who inherited millions.

George Williams was a millionaire. He was a bit more than a bit shady. He was suspected of laundering "unreported funds" for others. It was how he got his own. He had been associated with a group of thugs in the states.

His wife was Vera Karnes. That needed explanation.

Maybe not! She was Violet Kenneys when she married Williams. Elias had said it was sad, but she was all to pieces over the murder and unable to give any coherent testimony. She didn't have any ideas about who would want to harm George. He was a friend to everybody, though she was suspicious about a couple who seemed to be hiding something in their pasts. She didn't get involved in her husband's business.

A month later Elias quit for personal reasons and because he felt the job here was dead-end. He was popular with the people, but had never intended to be stuck with no chance of actual advancement.

A case where the wife or mistress of all the victims was probably the same person and he couldn't connect it? He didn't deserve advancement!

Alf sat back to consider. How inept was Elias, actually? Had he retired because he got a big gift from someone? A gift that was given because he didn't investigate a few little items?

Maybe a starting place would be to investigate Elias a bit. He could save enough in five years on the island detail to have a good cushion. There wasn't much to spend money on here. Add a gift of a few thousand and he could live fairly well for several years. Alf was planning on saving more than half his salary. So far, he it was looking like he could save almost all of it!

Alf had a date with Ilena, so asked her about Elias.

"He was alright. People liked him because he would turn his back on certain things, like you do.

I don't think he was gay, but he never dated any of us girls. He didn't seem to like men, so maybe he was just asexual. Some men are. There were stories that he had a woman – or man – on the mainland, not far from Capital City. He went there twice a month for one day. Jaime DeLeon saw him with a woman in Eastport in the city once. He said she was goodlooking if you like skinny women with big boobs. He wasn't sure they were together, but they seemed to be.

"Sis found some notes about ... well, private. I should shut up."

"No. This is important. It's about the four people murdered on Crab Island. I found a couple of things he should have seen. I have to know if he was just incompetent or if he maybe got paid not to see things."

"There were no bribes. He put two people here in jail for trying to bribe him about permits and things. He always had money. There wasn't anyplace to spend it. He said a lot of times that he was getting rich without half trying.

"I don't know much about investigations. He didn't seem incompetent to me, but Sis said he missed too much. It could be because he never did really understand the way people think here. He was too much a city person."

Yet he stayed here five years? I have to get a

little more on Officer Elias!

"Well, he's not here now, so maybe it doesn't matter. Those people who died were into some shady and downright illegal things.

"Want to go to Lily's? Paulo and Flo are playing some music tonight. They're always fun."

"Rico? I want to get some information about a cop. I'm turning up some strange things. The pieces aren't fitting so well."

"A cop? It would have to be Elias. He's the only one you would have any reason to want to know about.

"What? It's confidential if he was into something illegal."

"How good an investigator was he? Did he miss details in the academy? Would he overlook something from two cases that wouldn't mean anything in either one alone?"

"One of the cold cases? You've found something?"

"I think so. I don't think a trained investigator would miss it. How much experience did he have?"

"Like your own. None. Just the academy courses."

"If you had three cases where a major player was named Robert Martin in the first, Randy Moore in the second and Raul Mendez in the third, would you tend to want to know more about that man?"

There was a moment's silence. "So you've found a major part of three murders had a person with the same initials. I can assume that person was in a position to obscure evidence? Right?"

"Except for one thing."

"Which is?"

"Four cases."

"I need a couple of days to relax. I'm overdue for vacation. How's the fishing there?"

"You don't need a permit if you're not commercial. Tuna's in season. They're fun to catch."

"About nine in the morning. Got room at your place or is there a ... nothing there."

"Fold-out couch."

"Perfecto!"

"I can access his records from your computer. I have the codes," Rico explained. "I checked a little. It turns out he was married when he came here, but we didn't know it. We wouldn't send a married man to this kind of place."

"Wife's initials before she married him?"

"So! It was a woman's initials that you ... Vanys Parlaca."

"Does the term, 'Bingo!' mean anything to you?"

"Connect it!"

"Viviene Plato was mistress to victim one, Fethers. She inherited several million. Vanesa Partridge was married to victim two, Granger. She collected several million. Violet Pensión was married to victim three, Kenneys. She collected several millions. Vera Karnes was married to victim four, Williams. She collected several millions.

"Her initials would be V. K. when she married him because she was married to Kenneys. Probably had ID she could change a little with those initials.

"Now Elias was married to Vanys Parlaca all along, the original V. P.

"Well, Rookie Gomez," he said, in as condescending a tone as he could muster. "When you have a case where the same initials show up twice, you have a slight suspicion that it should be checked. When it happens a third time, you know damned well it needs attention. A fourth time and you have a very solid case. This is, counting Elias, five times. DUH!"

"So he has to be behind the whole mess. She or him or both."

"Uh-huh. It's a matter of proving it beyond the limits of what will be allowed in court, though that should be solid enough without anything further.

"I want to know if these were the first and only. That means a search and correlation program."

Rico nodded. He went to the computer and called up a program. He went through a list, selected a program, and downloaded it. "How far back?" he asked.

"Five years. I doubt there will be any before he got the assignment here. He or she or both found this was about perfect for making a few millions."

The computer search took more than four hours. It didn't come up with much. Rico went back through everything they had about Elias. Alf used his own laptop on the link to see what he could find about Vanys Parlaca. It was almost nothing.

He checked the other names she used. Very little. She stayed in the background.

"Well, I can't drop in on him. He would know it had something to do with my job," Rico complained. "I'd like to see how he's living these days!"

"I've never met him. Would he know ... I can do what she does. Use another name," Alf replied. "I think maybe I'll go calling on a man about the ... crap! I need a reason!"

"We know where she was at various times. Maybe we can connect something with one of the husbands. You could arrange to accidentally see her somewhere and scare the piss out of her."

Alf thought. An evil smirk came across his face. "Maybe an associate, connected, from when she was married to one of them will find it strange she's married the cop who investigated her dear husband's murder? Maybe the cop who took over the island office found a thing or two and asked about the wrong ... I'll have to make it one thing or another. I'll need a good story.

"Rico, do we have records of any of the people one of the husbands was running a scam with? Preferably someone who is dangerous as hell?"

Rico spent about fifteen minutes on the computer. He split the screen and drug items from the records to the new window. He ran it to printer. Alf took the sheets off and read them.

"And I'll be here, taking care of your job while you go to a family emergency."

Donald Granger, unofficial agent for UTD Properties, Investments and Paradise Perfect Land Developers, SA.

Donaldo Flores, Pres. UTD. Convicted fraud mj, 4 yrs. (5/2013). Ascd. Juan Salvatore, Sus. KFH.

Ernesto Galvajes, CEO PPLD. Sus. fraud, intmdt, vndlsm, mrdr(?)

Granger in meetings w/both several occsns. Salvatore ? 3/22/11 - 4/9/11 - 2/15/12 - 4/22/12 ?

Mar. V. P. 4/19/12

There was a lot more, but this was something he could use. They were all at a meeting three days after the wedding. She would have been close, but not at the meeting.

"Can you find where the meeting with Granger with Flores and Galvajes was?"

"Capital City. Let's see. In a restaurant. High-tower. Let me read the report. Flores was under surveillance. He went to the restaurant with Galvajes and Salvatore. The meeting with Granger may have been coincidence. He was there with his wife and his wife's mother and father. He went to the table of Flores to speak a moment, then back to his own table. He may have passed a paper to Flores. Uncertain."

"And I was a bodyguard for Galvajes who was sitting at a table between. Imagine my surprise when I saw Mrs. Granger at the market or something such! Imagine my further surprise that his wife was also the wife of the murdered man's police investigator! Real shock to find that Elias was the cop who investigated her husband's murder – and didn't find a clue!"

"Why, you filthy, slimy, no-good, rotten bastard, son of a bitch, blackmailer!"

"Nah-uh! A hired killer is never a blackmailer. That's a certain way to be sure you're the next one hit!

"Of course, things are a little rough right now.

"Oh, well! Just wanted to say, 'Hi!' I'll probably see you around. We can have a beer or two together for old time's sake!"

"You think he'll discuss things from the past?"

"No. He'll feel he has to repair that little dangerous thin spot."

"We'll have to make sure he can't knock you over before we can stop him."

"He's not the type to do anything himself. I want to know who else is involved – like who did the actual killing."

"It will be close. We can have a man or two close at all times."

"No. Elias was a cop. We can't be sure the killer or killers weren't also cops. I'll have to arrange it to where I can be reasonably safe. I don't plan to go after the killers, myself. I just want to identify them so the police can tag their asses, then I can disappear."

"Don't agree to take a boat trip to Crab Island."

"Crab Island? Why would anyone want to go to a place called Crab Island? Ugh!"

He got the finger for that one.

Alf asked around a number of places. First order was to find where Elias and wife were living. The address at the police station wasn't accurate. He had moved almost immediately after retiring.

He had millions, now. It would be a fancy section. He also liked the water.

The Yacht Club. Isla Esmeralda.

He wasn't there under his own name, but that was as much as expected. Alf had several pictures of Elias from the police information files. He wasn't very distinctive.

Well, he had a bit of money from the department. It was a legitimate investigation of murder. It was an investigation of a crooked cop at the same time.

Armitage Marcadore sauntered into the yacht club bar and sat at a table for two. He held up a hand for service. The pretty waitress in the skimpy outfit came. He ordered tequila and grapefruit juice with a touch of cloves. Tall and with lots of ice.

They would play hell finding powdered cloves,

probably. It wasn't a spice used in many drinks.

He looked around. Another pretty woman in a tight red dress raised an eyebrow. He returned. She came to sit across from him. She said, "Champagne." He said he would taste it to be sure they didn't give her Boone's Farm or something. She grinned and said, "No. They give me weak strawberry Flashade made with soda water."

He laughed. "So. How about a drink?"

"What're you having?"

"Tequila and grapefruit."

"Really? I've never tried that. It doesn't sound so great."

"I like it. A little cloves makes it really different and good."

"Okay. Why the hell not?"

He waved at the waitress and held up two fingers.

"So. New here?" she asked.

"You got to ask?"

She laughed. "Got to start somewhere."

"I'm just passing through. A friend said to try this place. I can meet a bunch of bigshits who are in hock up to their eyebrows. They'll bore me to death with tales about all their yachts and summer houses and jets and furs and jewels. They won't tell me about the mortgages on it all."

"So. We do have a few who are rich as Midas. Most of them are phony shits like you described. I charge two hundred. They want to put it on Visa because they're a little short of cash until they can get to the bank to release a million or two.

"I suppose you want to put it on Visa?"

"No way! I use Master Card!"

She laughed. "I think I like you. A hundred fifty."

"I'm not in the market at the moment. I'll buy the drinks and we can talk. Ilena doesn't care if I talk with other women. She gets a bit irate if I'm not in public when I do. She trusts me, but she doesn't trust other women.

"I thought I might run into Serg or his wife. If I'd known two days ago I'd be here I would have gotten his phone number or address or something."

"Sergio? I don't know of anyone named Sergio. What's his wife's name? Maybe I would know her."

"He calls her Veevee. I don't know if that's her name."

"I know of a Viviene. Maybe Veevee is a pet name. She's one of the richer of the rich. Her and her husband. Viviene ... what was it? She's ... Viviene Eladios. Her husband isn't Sergio, though. It's Sam."

Sam Eladios. Sergio Elias. Habits are hard to break. It was worth a shot. "She might have lived here for a couple of years. He was with some company that kept sending him all over the country or world or something."

"It could be her. Sam was here every couple of weeks for a day, then was gone again. Ship captain?"

"I did ... yes. He never said what he did, but he did talk about ships a lot.

"Do you know where I can find them? It could be him."

"They live over on the golf course. She plays tennis, he plays golf. Neither are very good at it. I don't see how someone as ordinary as him got someone who's a sex queen type to marry him. I would understand it if it was his money, but Barney – he's the club manager – checked and said most of it's in her name. It's old money, so if anyone married for money it would be him."

A group of men came in. She said, seeing he wasn't going to spend his hard-earned, she'd better get back to her job. Come see her when he got tired of the same old thing. He laughed and said that would be in about seventy years.

Okay. Viviene Eladios. Plays tennis. Sam plays golf. He might be able to set up something where he would logically have seen her. He could then manage to find where she lived and go calling.

He thought about it for a few minutes. It was altogether too possible Elias had seen his picture. He would have if he checked on who replaced him.

Alf wasn't very distinctive in pictures. A picture, such as the ones at the police, could be any of hundreds of people.

He got in touch with a friend who worked the streets. He would suddenly have a mustache. He was Latino enough that a bushy Mexican Brush would look almost normal. His eyebrows would also be bushy. That would change his looks more than the mustache.

He got a quick course on using disguises, then went to bed. Tomorrow was going to be an interesting day.

When he got up it was still dark. He had always been up early. He didn't sleep more than six hours a night, so went to bed late and got up early.

The restaurant opened at seven, but there was a 24 hour place a block away. He went to have a good breakfast and chat with the people there. He was staying in the cheaper part of the city. These were the real people.

He wasted a couple of hours, then headed for the club. He went to the tennis courts to look over the list of people and times. V. Eladios was tomorrow at ten AM. He wouldn't see her today.

He went to the golf course. S. Eladios teed off with R. Generoso, F. Herndon and C. Derwin at six thirty AM tomorrow.

So. What to do today?

He would rent a car to drive by the house. Elias could probably spot an unmarked. He'd worked long enough to know they were all the same make and model. Mitsubishis.

He went around the neighborhood to see the layout. The houses were secure and obviously expensive. Number 12 Calle Grande was very tasteful. There was, according to the neighborhood plan at the entrance, a pool behind. You looked from the terrace across the golf course to the Caribbean. Every house was on a two acre lot.

There was a BMW and a Lexus in the double carport.

There were stores and offices before the gated entrance to the neighborhood. They were, naturally, high-end. That meant something that cost five dollars in the regular stores cost twenty five there.

He decided to look around the shopping center. It didn't cost anything to look!

He was walking around awhile later past a fancy clothing store when the Lexus he'd seen at the house parked out front. A fairly pretty woman with an overdone shape got out to go into the store.

That was a break!

He waited until he saw her coming back out three quarters of an hour later and managed to be a few yards along the sidewalk. He smiled, then did a sort of doubletake, and said, "Mrs. Granger? Aren't you Mrs. Granger?"

She paled a little, recovered quickly, and said she had remarried. It was now Mrs. Eladios. Where did he know her from? She had a poor memory for faces. She didn't remember meeting him.

"Oh, we never met, directly. I was at the Hightower with, er, my boss one night. Ernesto Galvajes. You and Granger had just gotten married and happened to be there. I remember because Nesto said that you were one, uh, very attractive woman. He was jealous of Granger.

"You might not remember. Don Flores was there. He got his ass ... he got in trouble with the law not long after."

"I vaguely remember being in the Hightower a few times. You say just after I married ... oh, yes. Don said something about Donald seeing Donaldo in a restaurant and went to say he just got married.

"I really have to get to an appointment. Nice seeing you."

"Equal," he replied. She got in the car and drove away.

She was trying hard not to show how shook up she was. Now he could run into Elias on the golf course. He would mention that he met the wife at the store. He remembered her from when she was married to that guy who got offed. See what kind of reaction that got!

This might get interesting. Hairy, but interesting.

Alf was at the pro shop when Elias and three other men came in. He seemed a bit distracted. He was saying his wife had met a person from his past. A person he never wanted to see again.

Alf stayed out of sight while they signed in and put their clubs on a golf cart. They headed for the tee. He waited. He was about to happen by when he thought better of it. He would wait. They were playing nine holes, so would be through about ten thirty.

Viviene would be playing tennis about then. Might be fun to see if she made a call if she happened to see him in the club. It would be coffee time.

He went into town to return at a quarter to ten. She was in the restaurant with another woman. He went by where she got a good look at him, but didn't glance in her direction. She saw him and put a menu in front of her face until he was past. He could see that in the mirrored stanchions at the restaurant entrance. He went on to the restroom. When he got back out she was talking on her cellular. He didn't look her way and went back into the clubhouse.

He waited. She went to the courts and started playing tennis with the woman who was with her at the restaurant. Elias didn't come by, but a man did come to chat with her for a minute. The man looked familiar.

Alf used his phone to take a picture of him with her. It was clear on zoom. They could easily be identified from it.

The man soon left. She went back onto the courts.

Alf went to the police station and back to Rico's office. The secretary had orders about him. He got mug shots on the computer and spent a long time looking, coming up with zilch.

He asked the secretary if she could find who this one was. He showed her the pictures he had downloaded.

"I know who he is. Franco Bernadetti. Bad news. Arranges things. He doesn't do anything, himself, so we can't prove anything."

He thought a bit, then brought up known and suspected associates of Franco Bernadetti. He got pictures and short notes about eleven different people, four of whom were suspected hit men (though one hit "man" was a woman). He would be looking over his shoulder for that bunch, for certain.

He had a provable connection with Viviene. If they could place any of those people in the islands on certain dates they had a solid case waiting. It would be a real charge to take someone like Bernadetti down along with his own case.

He went through hundreds of pages about Bernadetti. He had some big politicians in his pocket. He wasn't going down, but they may be able to take down some of his "contractors" with this.

He saw an article he put to the side, went on until he'd done a cursory on all pages, then went to the selected one.

He had wondered all along why Crab Island. If the bodies had been spread around different islands they probably wouldn't have caught his attention. Crab Island was a mangrove head. There could never be any development there, even if it had other features, which it didn't seem to have. This was an article on an internet site about a sale of private islands. It was included in the information about Bernadetti because he was president of a company that bought (?) three islands in the bay.

That question mark was because there was no record of the sale to Bernadetti.

Alf went to the title information for that area.

The title on record said the land belonged to John Forester Headly, resident, citizen of Canada. There was a tag on the title that said it was under question to be resolved if there were any other sales including the property.

Why didn't they simply contact Headly and ask him if there was a transfer? If he said, "No," Bernadetti couldn't sell it. Bernadetti was attempting to sell it on that site.

The site was four years old. Bernadetti had an unregistered title from six years ago. Headly had supposedly signed the property over to Bernadetti in repayment of a loan.

Again: Why not contact Headly?

Alf went to the net to Google Headly. Very little. He was a semi-wealthy man who had retired from a transportation business he sold to an international container business. He was 55 years old when he retired with something over three quarters of a million dollars, Canadian.

He was, after consulting the net, now 69 years old.

Google didn't have anything nearly complete. He went to Yahoo! Headly had disappeared six years ago. He was supposedly a recluse in a foreign country. A brother said he showed some early signs of Alzheimer's Disease when he retired. None of the family had contact with him.

He had always been a loner.

He checked immigration. Headly had residence from seven years ago. He was in and out of the country until almost six years ago. His address was 12 Calle Grande, Capital City.

Headly had that island. He was living where Elias and loving spouse were now living. He had disappeared about the time Elias took over the job of patrolman in the area of Crab Island.

Was the lovely Viviene Headly's wife before she met Elias – or after, for that matter?

He went back to the title registro.

Headly still owned the house. His wife had filed for title when he disappeared. She would have to wait seven years. That would be in less than two years.

Alf called Rico. He said Headly's body might be in the cold cases. He had a file on the net under coded information that explained what he thought had happened.

He made notes on the information sheet while Rico checked the cold cases. None of them were murders.

"Rico, I'll put this thing on hold here. I'll be back there this afternoon. I want to go over Crab Island inch by inch. We may be able to tie this bunch up tight!"

"What do you mean?"

"I'm not sure. Maybe we can get a heinous murder charge against Franco Bernadetti."

There was a silence. "Bernadetti? Not a chance. If you could do that you'd be my boss next week. Police commissioner for life! Cop hero of the decade!"

"If what I think happened turns out to be what happened, he can't entirely escape. Maybe not *the* big one, but *a* big one ... or ten."

He soon rang off and headed for his hotel. He would leave some things there. He might be back as soon as tomorrow.

He had the chopper deliver him to the islands. He and Rico took the new launch out to head for Crab Island at dawn the following day.

Alf beached the boat at one of the spots where there was a way into the interior. He and Rico took machetes. He knew his way through mangroves. He had to teach Rico a few things.

They explored to the center of the island. Nothing but rocks and swamp and mangroves.

He moved to the next spot. They explored until it started getting dark.

The following morning they returned to where they left the day before. Two hours later Rico called that he found something odd. Alf made his way to him. He was standing by a pile of rocks on a sandy rise. There was sawgrass growing among the rocks.

"You see what I see?" Rico asked.

"Yeah. Sawgrass grows where there's organic material below. It doesn't do well in sand. There's something under those rocks that's feeding it. You can see by the older growth that it's a lot smaller and poorer now than a couple of years ago. The food source is almost all used up.

"I think we'll find what's left of Headly's body under there. I hope there will be enough to identify."

They took pictures and loran numbers, then began moving rocks. It wasn't an easy task, but they soon found bones.

"I hope to hell we can get positive ID from what's here. We know who it was, but can we prove it?" Rico said.

"I think definitely so. Look at the skull. The teeth."

There were implanted teeth screwed into the jawbone and upper bone.

"Better than any fucking fingerprint!" Rico exulted.

If they had been anywhere it would be practical they would call in a forensics crew. Here, that wasn't possible. They spent the rest of the day very carefully bagging the skeleton and articles found with it. There was a plastic case in a pocket of the pants the skeleton was wearing. It had a passport and some papers, an ATM card, and some notes in a little calendar notebook.

"We open that case at the office with witnesses and pictures and audio and the whole schmeer," Alf said. "I'm praying to a god I don't believe in that notebook has something about a meeting at Crab Island with Franco Bernadetti!"

"One chance in ten million, but I'm with you, there!"

They got to the dock as the sun sank below the mountains on the mainland. They took until nine thirty to carefully move everything they had into the office closet. Alf locked the place tighter than it had ever been locked before.

Then they went to bed.

At dawn they had Ilena, Tina and Teresa there with Santo and Carlos Gerente, two of the local fishermen. They very carefully went through the bones and so forth. Teresa said there was something, something metal, against the spine. Lodged in it, actually.

It was a bullet. A .38 or .40 caliber. Brass jacket. Very clear ballistic print.

"Ladies and gentlemen and undecideds, we have here the object that caused the death by murder of John Forester Headly. Matched to the specific pistol of blank, we have proof of murder by deadly weapon," Alf announced.

"Thank you, Jesus!" Rico cried.

They finished the examination, then turned to the articles found with the body. The deteriorated clothing was photographed and listed, then the articles otherwise associated with the body.

"A leather billfold containing what's left of four twenty dollar bills, one five, three ones. A plastic encapsulated Social Services card. An ATM card for Bank of Canada and one for Banco General here. Both are Visa debit cards also.

"Several photographs in plastic carriers. One is of a woman I can personally identify as a woman now calling herself Viviene Eladios, but who was his wife. She was the wife of several other murdered people.

"A clip with a small electric lantern on a key-chain with four keys.

"Two quarters, a dime and two nickels found under the body.

"A card case with sixteen business cards from various places and nine of the victim's personal cards.

"A plastic case containing, from open viewing, a passport and various papers and a notebook.

"A small penknife and a Swiss Army Knife.

"A Bulova wristwatch. A wedding band, gold. A signet ring from Loyola Universtiy.

"We will now open the plastic case.

"The passport in the name of John Forester Headly. Canada.

"A bankbook from Banco General. More than six hundred thousand dollars. Six hundred four thousand three hundred ten dollars and fifty two cents.

"Notes. *Meet Mariam at Hightower four PM seventh.*

Franco B. Noon. Eighth

Lettuce, tomatoes, Ranch Dressing, bacon.

"There is a calendar notebook."

Rico removed the notebook, took a deep breath, and looked inside.

"This is the property of J. F. Headly, 12 Calle Grande, Capital City. Two cell phone numbers and a home phone number.

"It starts with July 1st, 2008. The pages before were cut out.

"Page two. Oswaldo. four Pm. Dinner V and mother, Hightower, seven thirty

"Page three. Golf. G at office. noon.

"Page four. V at Enrique's (ugh) two PM

"Page five. F. B. 555-0044. CI

"Page six: blank. He started making longer notes, almost like a diary here.

"Page seven: V and B. What are they up to? Who is Serg?

"Page eight: Island sold. B. Need to wait.

"Pages nine and ten blank

"Page eleven: Sergio V's cousin. V has a habit of lying, so I don't know."

He rifled through until near the end. "I think this will be the important part. It's September nine.

"F wants island. V and he too chummy. Got to be careful. She can scheme."

He went a couple of pages more.

"September eleven. Franco Bernadetti scares me. Going to island tomorrow. V going along. I'll see if this is a scam. I arranged for the policeman there to go with us.

"That's the last entry."

"So! She was working with Bernadetti. We have them both cold for premeditated murder."

"The team from Capital City will be here in half an hour to take this evidence back. I'll also go back. I want to drop in to say hello to the ex-cop here and his lovely wife," Alf said.. "He was with them. Three for murder. Firing squad here."

Rico saluted.

"Hi! I saw your wife at the shopping center and decided to drop in. Here I am!"

Elias stared at him. "You are?"

"Your replacement in Aguas Verdes. We found Headly's body. That, and a few other little items.

"Bernadetti around, or keeping his distance?"

Elias got a very hard look. "So. How much?"

"They haven't printed that much yet. Viviene, Violet, Vanys and whatever else home?"

Elias reached behind his back and came out with a pistol. Alf grinned. He had his own pointed directly at Elias' crotch.

"Drop it or I shoot you where you'll wish I'd killed you."

He dropped it.

"What lousy manners! Aren't you going to invite me and my friends in?" He waved at the six-man squad coming in from the front with automatic weapons trained on Elias. Rico came from behind to say, "Hello, Serg! Long time, no see!"

Elias sobbed and stood back. Viviene came just then to say, "Who was ... what is going on here?"

"I just dropped in to charge you and you spouse with premeditated murder, five counts and investigations continuing," Alf replied. "You want to call Bernadetti? A squad is arresting him right about now."

She looked from him to Alf to the squad.

She fainted.

"Officer Mercedes," Judge Moritos called. "Testimony. Questions allowed."

The court system here was different from many places. Alf would give his testimony in essay fashion, then the prosecution or defense could question him. Bernadetti had a team of lawyers who were from other places. They had already tried to claim technicalities. Moritos had said, "So what?" to most of them. They tried to exclude things found at the scene because there was no specialist team to see the evidence chain was unbroken. Moritos looked at the videos with audio and said, "Where?"

They argued that things weren't identified properly at the scene and blah, blah, blah. Moritos told them to get it together. If they wished to challenge a specific piece of evidence, do so at the proper time. Any more stalling attempts and they would be found incompetent and not knowledgeable about law in this place. He didn't have the time for theatricality.

Next was trying to get the defense divided into two or three cases, letting Bernadetti have a way to disconnect the case. No way! They were charged with murder by committee and were all charged with being at the scene of the first murder. It was a single case against three defendants to be held equally guilty or innocent.

"It started when I was looking through the cold case files. I noticed that a woman was involved in each case. A woman with the same initials. V. P.

"That was unusual in three cases, but here were four. It was beyond coincidence, so I ..."

"Question!" a defense lawyer shouted.

"Just say you have a question. Don't shout. This ain't no druggie movie. What?"

"Insufficient evidence to begin an investigation. Does the witness mean to imply that any case where someone with the same initials appears is suspicious?"

"No," Moritos answered, before Alf could say anything. "He implies that any five cases with that happening is suspicious. Irrelevant.

"Another thing. What difference could it possibly make why an investigation was started? If it leads to capture of criminals, who cares why there was an investigation. Maybe the officer had a headache and was in a bad mood. So what? Continue."

"It seemed odd that the officer in charge of the investigation of those murders didn't catch that point, so a suspicion began that he was crooked or incompetent. That could wait until something was discovered about murder.

"Rather obviously, the first consideration was whether or not the same woman was involved. If so, she would be the primary suspect for causing the murders. She wouldn't necessarily be suspected of chopping four people up with a machete.

"The fifth – actually, the first victim, was shot. It doesn't make any difference if she fired the shot. She was there and was behind the scheme."

"Question!"

Moritos sighed. "What?"

"It doesn't make any difference who fired a fatal shot? Really?"

Moritos shook his head. "No, it makes no difference. This was murder by committee. All are equally guilty. Really! Continue."

"Protest! Judge biased against defense!"

"For explaining the law? You, sir, are incompetent to be here in your capacity. You rather obviously do not know the law as enforced here. One more such silly outburst and you will be expelled from these proceedings. Clear?"

He looked confused. The lawyer sitting next to him pulled him down into the seat. Moritos pointed to Alf.

"That investigation led to the fact that it was, indeed, the same woman. She had been mistress to one victim and wife to three. Later, it was found that she was married all the time to Officer Elias, the officer who did not investigate the initial connection. It was easy to conjecture why."

"Question! That cop just said he based his case on *conjecture*? I don't believe it!"

"Bailiff! Get that incompetent moronic ass out of my courtroom! This is no silly TV movie set! This is a trial of capital case against three people! It is *not* a game!

"Continue."

Alf almost couldn't hide the grin. "I then called in my superior officer, Enrique Gomez, to aid in pursuing the investigation. We compared notes and studied the evidence and older testimony. We decided it would serve well for me to come here to Capital City to find the suspects and determine if they were, as suspected, in some kind of conspiracy to gain some tens of millions of dollars through murder.

"During that investigation Franco Bernadetti was brought into focus. It puzzled me why the woman even knew of him.

"I then discovered that Mr. Headly, while married to the woman in question, was drawn into a scam over sale of Crab Island, the place where

Officer Gomez and I found the remains of Mr. Headly.

"When we read that note in the papers, we saw the entire scheme for what it was."

"Question! Would Officer Mercedes please connect the chronology of this case a bit more clearly? We have jumped from finding a piece of paper to Mr. Bernadetti being charged with murder. Too much is left out of that equation."

"Agreed," Moritos replied. "Officer Mercedes, a little more clarity?"

"Yes, Your Honor. I have jumped too far ahead without connecting facts.

"Franco Bernadetti was mentioned as having been in several places at the same time as the victims. We are well aware of Mr. Bernadetti's reputation, but didn't really connect him until he was seen conversing with the woman at a tennis court. It was immediately after I had spoken to the woman, seeming to know she was at a meeting among her husband and known gangsters.

"Mr. Bernadetti is suspected of arranging what we call 'hits' in police parlance. We had four bodies we knew of and suspected others. The woman wasn't where most of those murders took place. Mr. Bernadetti is known, or seriously suspected, to arrange such things.

"Two and two is four. A woman connected

through false marriages to victims and a hit man were the obvious thing to investigate. We did.

"I will try to say some things I realize I have not stated here. One is why Crab Island was the point of four murders was a consideration even before the woman's initials were connected. There is nothing there. It is a mangrove head. Had other locations been used, I probably wouldn't have made the connection with the initials. Four murders in four places would tend to seem unconnected. Crab Island was the connection on which I based the initial investigation, then the importance of those initials became obvious.

"I traced to ownership of the island, of course. Mr. Bernadetti's connection came into focus because he was involved in a plan to sell the island. That led to how he could sell an island he didn't own. The title was still in the name of Headly. Then I met the woman of the initials. Then Mr. Bernadetti met with her. I had known he was in on a scheme to sell Crab Island from an advertisement on the internet. I saw the place, then found that it was the woman whose initials I was investigating who was living there, she had been married to Headly, she was now married to the officer who didn't find any evidence in four murders. Headly had disappeared.

"Now the island, woman, officer, and Bernadetti

were all coming together. I had always wondered why Crab Island. Here was the connection.

"Headly had mysteriously disappeared soon after the officer was assigned that duty. He was married to the woman at the time. Bernadetti was trying to sell the island he didn't own.

"I suspected the island was more important than we knew, but how? Why?

"We knew of four bodies at that time. Headly had disappeared at the time before the first body was found. I suspected the importance of that island was because Headly was actually the first murdered there. The others were lured there by some kind of phony sales pitch.

"Officer Gomez and I went to the island to search it minutely. We found Headly's body. It was easy to find a positive. He had extensive and unique dental work. There was zero doubt the body we discovered was, indeed, John Forester Headly.

"As shown on the videos and photos, we discovered an undeniable connection with Mr. Bernadetti, Sergio Elias, Elias's wife, Viviene. It was noted in his calendar book that he was meeting them on Crab Island. Elias was there, he thought, for his protection. That was the last entry into the notebook.

"We made the arrests. The gun, a Glock forty,

was found at the estate of Mr. Headly. We can't show who fired the shot, but that is of no concern here. All three were there for the sole purpose of killing John Forester Headly. They accomplished that goal. They are equally guilty of premeditated murder, in my personal opinion."

"Thank you, Officer Mercedes. Any questions? Make them relevant."

"Chronology," the prosecutor said. "Please list the factors in order that you have explained here."

"I was bored. I went through the cold case files. I discovered there were four murders on Crab Island. I discovered the woman with the same initials was involved in all four murders. I found the officer involved in the investigation had missed such an obvious clue. I investigated and discovered a man named Headly owned the island. I discovered Mr. Bernadetti was trying to sell the island. I discovered Mr. Headly was missing for four years. I discovered officer Elias was married to a woman with the same initials, had been all along. I found that the woman with the initials was Headfly's wife, that it was Headly's house she and Officer Elias were occupying. I came here to the city to investigate the woman and Elias. I caused the woman to contact Mr. Bernadetti. I developed a suspicion that the reason Crab Island was so involved was because Headly's body was on it. Officer Gomez and I discovered that body. There was a notebook that put Mr. Bernadetti, Officer Elias and his wife, Viviene, at the scene of the murder. We arrested all three and charged them with, as Your Honor stated, murder by committee."

"Thank you. Defense?"

"Defense will appeal. The connections in Officer Mercedes' mind were not solidified in this testimony."

"Question!" Alf cried.

"From the ... yes?" from Moritos.

"You Honor has not yet ruled. The defense announces it will appeal. Could the defense please clarify the chronology of that factor?"

Moritos laughed. "I suppose that was because the fact that your case is not one where there is any doubt made it obvious that I would have to rule this as conspiracy murder, or murder by committee. Five counts.

"So stated. Sentencing tomorrow at nine o'clock AM. You will also know what the sentence will be. I also have no choice in that.

"Without further?"

There were no further questions. "Court's adjourned."

They filed out.

"Murder, premeditated, is proven. There is evidence in two cases of torture. That makes it heinous. All three defendants participated directly in at least one murder. Sentence is proscribed. Death by firing squad. Ten days from this moment.

"Appeal was stated by defense at trial. It is also automatic.

"So stated. Court is adjourned."

They filed out. Alf was to head back to the islands. Rico was headed back to his office.

Alf would leave for the island in the chopper tomorrow. Ilena and he would spend the night in the city. Alf would show her off at the Hightower.

It was a very pleasant time. Alf would have to be at the appeals court, though he may not be called.

Gomez called to say that something was up. Bernadetti was almost smug. He seemed to have it set up that he would get away with it.

Alf remembered the political connections he found when he investigated Bernadetti. He told Gomez what was almost certain to happen. A judge was bought off. On the Supreme Court.

He also remembered something about the law here. He called the Prensa Diario to say he had something to discuss about the Bernadetti case. He had been asked to attend an interview, but had declined because the police were discouraged from such things, but this was important to the people and the reputation of the country.

He was asked to come to the TV station for a direct broadcast on "Your opinion!" The printed media were always there to ask questions. It was a politically directed show that was hard on corruption.

He showed up at the time and went directly to the stage. The woman who would moderate asked what it was to be about. That the murders were a part of it was a given. Were there questions that should be asked or avoided?

"No. I mainly want to make a statement about the law, about how it is slanted to let politically connected people get away with serious crimes, even murder. It is about something in the constitution that is almost never mentioned, but it is there."

She studied him for a minute. "You're going to start a firestorm on my program, aren't you?"

"If I can."

"Great! Go for it!"

He was led to a seat across a kidney-shaped table. The cameraman counted, "Five, four, three, two, one!" and pointed to Gloria Suarez, the moderator.

"Good morning. The guests scheduled for this segment are waiting until Officer Mercedes, of the recent multiple murder case so much in the news, makes a statement. We will try to make it short enough that Dr. Amos and Councilman Dorada can appear as scheduled.

"Officer Mercedes, the floor is yours."

"Thank you, Gloria. I will be as brief as possible. What I have to say is really very simple.

"The case in which I was involved recently has been appealed to the Supreme Court, as is declared by law. It is expected and proper. It will correct wrongs, when applied properly.

"The constitution states that these proceedings can be held in closed court unless there is reason and demand from the people to hold it in open court.

"One of the defendants is known to be connected to major political figures, some not of a type to garner much confidence."

Gloria rolled her eyes and giggled. There was a murmur of laughter from the fifty or so in the audience.

"I think this case should be a demand case, where the proceedings are public. I think those proceedings should be broadcast on this channel and printed in the press.

"A judge, under those conditions, cannot give a written explanation to be held in a restricted file that he released a prisoner because the trial was tainted, that the prosecutor went too far or something as transparent. He or she will have to give an explanation right then and there to the public. In this case, there are no grounds for appeal. It is done because it is automatic in capital cases.

"There have been cases as strong that were overturned on a silly technicality you have not been allowed to read. Your laughter about the confidence in the courts tells me you have had enough of this travesty.

"This is one case, but *you* may demand it in any case you feel would fail due to corruption or intimidation.

"It is time it *stopped*!

"Thank you Gloria. I feel strongly about this."

"As do I! I call for immediate petition! You may go to the internet to the address on the bottom of the screen and may register your demand. Written petition will be circulated here. People watching can print out a form that simply says you demand public exposure of the case against the Crab Island Murderers. The case number and time are just now appearing on the bottom of the screen.

"People! Friends of law and liberty! Alf is right! It is time this travesty *stops*!"

"Thank you, Gloria. I feel the courts here in Capital City have been used too much, that this hurts every single person in this land. To end it is too much to ask, but we can make progress one case at a time until the courts are peopled by actual caring people who feel honor in the courts is needed to allow pride in our country.

"This country has much to be proud of!"

A man brought out a meter that numbered the hits on the petition on the net. There were already more than a thousand signatures. The secondary law said two thousand five hundred or more may not be ignored.

Gloria said they would have ten times that in fifteen minutes!

She was right. Alf went back to the hotel. In a couple of hours, the islands. Home!

<u>*Life Goes On*</u>

Alf stretched and put the coffee on. Ilena came in from in back with eggs from the chickens running around the place. She said she had sliced ham and pineapple she would heat up with the eggs.

"The Supreme Court will be on TV with your case at eleven. Two judges have protested public exposure, but they can't stop it. It will get very serious, very quickly."

Alf smiled at her. "I can picture two reactions. One is fast and good, one is slow and will lead to exposure of more than the case.

"I'll take a quick run to Esmeralda and back. I should be back here at eleven."

They talked about various things. Tina would marry Carlos Sunday. Seeing they had been living together for a year, it wouldn't be a big deal. She was pregnant and religious, so wanted the baby born under the blessings of the church.

Alf made the run. Nothing was happening at Esmeralda that needed his attention. He got back ten minutes before the broadcast. Ilena called that they were making a big deal of it.

He went in to see hundreds of people marching outside the courthouse. They were demanding public participation in the choosing of justices. It had been too long going on when a politician selected a judge and other politicians approved them, then they couldn't get rid of them.

The time for the appeal case came. The courtroom was shown with capacity seating filled. Reporters were standing around and on the mezzanine.

The nine judges filed in and sat. Supreme Judge Salvatores rapped the gavel.

"Order. Seats and silence.

"We are here to consider case M four seventy five hyphen sixty two H forty seven. It is labeled the Crab Island Murder Case in public forums.

"We have studied the videos and printed proceedings and have little question. If there are any points to consider by this panel?" He looked around. No one turned on the attention light.

"Very well. We find no cause to alter or overturn the rulings of the lower court. Proper proceedings were noted. We find the appeal by the counsel of the defendants to be without basis.

"Sentence stands.

"If there are no further tasks we need ponder?" No reaction.

"Court adjourned."

The audience – and Alf – applauded wildly. The finding was announced outside. People were dancing and applauding.

"Well! The last solution I expected! The easy way out!" Alf declared.

"Do you want to look at some more of the cold case files?" Teresa, who had come to watch the proceedings, asked.

"No."

C. D. Moulton's works are available on most major outlets as printed or e-books. CD writes the CD Grimes, PI, mysteries, the Det. Lt. Nick Storie mysteries, the Clint Faraday mysteries, the Flight of the Maita science fiction series, books on orchid culture and many others of many types. Mystery, adventure, intrigue, science fiction, humor, fantasy, paranormal, mild erotica, and factual.